CYNDY SZEKERES'

Mother Goose Rhymes

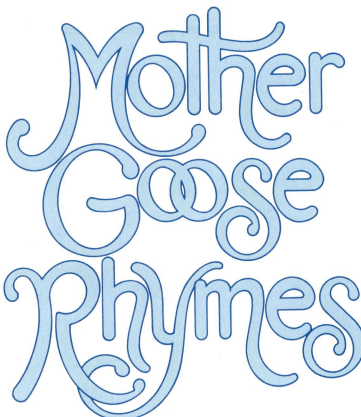

Selected and illustrated by Cyndy Szekeres

A GOLDEN BOOK • NEW YORK
Western Publishing Company, Inc.
Racine, Wisconsin 53404

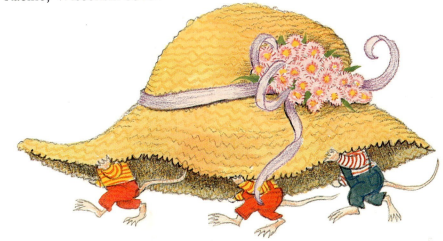

A NOTE FROM THE ARTIST

I believe that children thrive on an abundance of love and affection, and this belief has guided my selection of Mother Goose rhymes and the version chosen for each rhyme. I dedicate this book to all children, with the hope that their lives may be filled with love and happiness.

Cyndy Szekeres

Library of Congress Cataloging-in-Publication Data

Mother Goose.
    Cyndy Szekeres' Mother Goose rhymes.

    Summary: An illustrated collection of traditional
nursery rhymes.
    1. Nursery rhymes.   2. Children's poetry.
[1. Nursery rhymes]   I. Szekeres, Cyndy, ill.
II. Title.   III. Title: Mother Goose rhymes.
PZ8.3.M85 1987   398'.8   84-81596
ISBN: 0-307-15560-9
ISBN: 0-307-65560-1 (lib. binding)

TABLE OF CONTENTS

Cackle, cackle, Mother Goose,
Have you any feathers loose?
Truly have I, pretty fellow,
Half enough to fill a pillow.
Here are quills, take one or two,
And down to make a bed for you.

Cock crows in the morn
    To tell us to rise,
And he who lies late
    Will never be wise;
For early to bed
    And early to rise,
Is the way to be healthy
    And wealthy and wise.

Cock a doodle doo!
My dame has lost her shoe;
My master's lost his fiddlestick
And knows not what to do.

1, 2, buckle my shoe;

3, 4, shut the door;

5, 6, pick up sticks;

7, 8, lay them straight;

9, 10, a good fat hen;

11, 12, I hope you're well;

13, 14, draw the curtain;

15, 16, the maid's in the kitchen;

17, 18, she's in waiting;

19, 20, my stomach's empty.

Rub-a-dub-dub, three men in a tub,
   And who do you think they be?
The butcher, the baker, the candlestick-maker,
   And all of them going to sea.

Little Bo-peep has lost her sheep
And can't tell where to find them;
Leave them alone, and they'll come home,
And bring their tails behind them.

Baa, baa, black sheep,
    Have you any wool?
Yes, sir, yes, sir,
    Three bags full;

One for the master,
    And one for the dame,
And one for the little boy
    Who lives down the lane.

12

Mary had a little lamb,
Its fleece was white as snow;
And everywhere that Mary went
The lamb was sure to go.

It followed her to school one day,
That was against the rule;
It made the children laugh and play
To see a lamb at school.

And so the teacher turned it out,
But still it lingered near,
And waited patiently about
Till Mary did appear.

''Why does the lamb love Mary so?''
The eager children cry.
''Why, Mary loves the lamb, you know,''
The teacher did reply.

14

I saw a ship a-sailing,
    A-sailing on the sea;
And, oh, but it was laden
    With pretty things for thee.

There were comfits in the cabin,
    And apples in the hold;
The sails were made of silk,
    And the masts were all of gold.

The four-and-twenty sailors
    That stood between the decks,
Were four-and-twenty white mice
    With chains about their necks.

The captain was a duck,
    With a packet on his back,
And when the ship began to move,
    The captain said, "Quack, quack!"

Pat-a-cake, pat-a-cake,
    Baker's man,
Bake me a cake
    As fast as you can.
Pat it, and prick it,
    And mark it with B,
And put it in the oven
    For Baby and me.

Hot-cross buns!
Hot-cross buns!
One a penny, two a penny,
Hot-cross buns!

If your daughters do not like them,
Give them to your sons.
One a penny, two a penny,
Hot-cross buns!

Pease porridge hot,
Pease porridge cold,
Pease porridge in the pot
Nine days old.
Some like it hot,
Some like it cold,
Some like it in the pot
Nine days old.

Hush, baby, my dolly,
    I pray you don't cry,
And I'll give you some bread,
    And some milk by and by;
Or perhaps you like custard,
    Or maybe a tart?
Then to either you're welcome,
    With all my heart.

Handy-spandy, Jack-a-dandy,
Loves plum cake and sugar candy.
He bought some at a grocer's shop,
And, pleased, away went hop, hop, hop.

Jack, be nimble, Jack, be quick;
Jack, jump over the candlestick.

Jack Sprat could eat no fat,
  His wife could eat no lean,
And so between them both, you see,
  They licked the platter clean.

Jack and Jill went up the hill
  To fetch a pail of water;
Jack fell down and broke his crown,
  And Jill came tumbling after.

Little Miss Muffet
Sat on a tuffet,
Eating her curds and whey;
There came a big spider,
Who sat down beside her,
And frightened Miss Muffet away.

Little Tom Tucker
Sings for his supper.
What shall he eat?
White bread and butter.
How will he cut it
Without e'er a knife?
How will he be married
Without e'er a wife?

Little Jack Horner
Sat in a corner,
Eating a Christmas pie;
He put in his thumb,
And pulled out a plum,
And said, "What a good boy am I!"

There was a little girl who had a little curl
Right in the middle of her forehead;
When she was good, she was very, very good,
But when she was bad she was horrid.

Lucy Locket lost her pocket,
Kitty Fisher found it;
There was not a penny in it,
But a ribbon round it.

Peter Piper picked a peck of pickled peppers;
A peck of pickled peppers Peter Piper picked.
If Peter Piper picked a peck of pickled peppers,
Where's the peck of pickled peppers Peter Piper picked?

Rain, rain, go away,
Come again another day,
Little Johnny wants to play.

Peter, Peter, pumpkin eater,
Had a wife and couldn't keep her;
He put her in a pumpkin shell,
And there he kept her very well.

There was an old woman tossed in a blanket
    Seventeen times as high as the moon;
But where she was going no mortal could tell,
    For under her arm she carried a broom.

"Old woman, old woman, old woman," said I,
    "Whither, ah whither, ah whither so high?"
"To sweep the cobwebs from the sky,
    And I'll be with you by and by."

Hey diddle, diddle,
    The cat played the fiddle,
The cow jumped over the moon.
    The little dog laughed
    To see such a sport,
And the dish ran away with the spoon.

There was an old woman
    Who lived in a shoe,
She had so many children
    She didn't know what to do.
She gave them some broth
    Without any bread,
She hugged them and kissed them
    And put them to bed.

Here am I, little jumping Joan,
When nobody's with me
I'm always alone.

Old Mother Hubbard went to the cupboard
To fetch her poor dog a bone;
But when she got there, the cupboard was bare,
And so her poor dog had none.

Bow, wow, wow!
Whose dog art thou?
Little Tom Tinker's dog,
Bow, wow, wow!

Old Mistress McShuttle
Lived in a coal-scuttle,
Along with her dog and her cat;
What they ate I can't tell,
But 'tis known very well,
That none of the party was fat.

Old King Cole
Was a merry old soul,
And a merry old soul was he;
He called for his pipe,
And he called for his bowl,
And he called for his fiddlers three.

Humpty Dumpty sat on a wall,
Humpty Dumpty had a great fall;
All the king's horses, and all the king's men,
Couldn't put Humpty together again.

35

March winds and April showers
Bring forth May flowers.

In April's sweet month,
When the leaves 'gin to spring,
Little lambs skip like fairies
And birds build and sing.

One misty, moisty morning,
When cloudy was the weather,
I chanced to meet an old man clothed all in leather.
He began to compliment, and I began to grin,
How do you do, how do you do?
And how do you do again?

Thirty days hath September,
April, June, and November;
All the rest have thirty-one,
Excepting February alone,
And that has twenty-eight days clear
And twenty-nine in each leap year.

Rock-a-bye, baby,
On the treetop,
When the wind blows,
The cradle will rock.
When the bough breaks,
The cradle will fall,
And down will come baby,
Cradle, and all.

A wise old owl sat in an oak,
The more he heard the less he spoke;
The less he spoke the more he heard.
Why aren't we all like that wise old bird?

A diller, a dollar,
A ten o'clock scholar,
What makes you come so soon?
You used to come at ten o'clock,
But now you come at noon!

Ride a cock-horse
    To Banbury Cross,
To see a fine lady
    Upon a white horse;
With rings on her fingers
    And bells on her toes,
She shall have music
    Wherever she goes.

When I was a little he,
My mother took me on her knee,
Smiles and kisses gave with joy,
And called me oft her darling boy.

Doctor Foster went to Gloucester,
In a shower of rain;
He stepped in a puddle, right up to his middle,
And never went there again.

Smiling girls, rosy boys,
Come and buy my little toys;
Monkeys made of gingerbread,
And sugar horses painted red.

Little Boy Blue,
　　Come blow your horn,
The sheep's in the meadow,
　　The cow's in the corn.

Where is the boy
　　Who looks after the sheep?
He's under a haycock
　　Fast asleep.

Hickory, dickory, dock,
The mouse ran up the clock;
The clock struck one,
The mouse ran down,
Hickory, dickory, dock.

Diddle, diddle, dumpling, my son John
Went to bed with his trousers on;
One shoe off and one shoe on,
Diddle, diddle, dumpling, my son John.

Wee Willie Winkie
    Runs through the town,
Upstairs and downstairs,
    In his nightgown;
Tapping at the window,
    Crying at the lock;
"Are the children in their beds,
    For it's now eight o'clock?"